Pizza-Pie Snowman

Valeri Gorbachev

Holiday House / New York

Pinky had a job to do for Mommy—to get a pizza with all their favorite toppings. He made a poem so he wouldn't forget:

Mushrooms, mozzarella cheese,
Fresh tomatoes, onions, peas.

All of a sudden . . .

BOP!

A snowball hit Pinky on the head.

Pinky's friends the Squirrel boys were throwing snowballs from their tree.

"Play with us," they said.

"Can't," said Pinky. "I'm getting a pizza for my mommy."

Mushrooms, mozzarella cheese,
Fresh tomatoes, onions, peas.

But the Squirrel boys weren't listening. **BOP!** Another snowball hit Pinky on the head.

"STOP!" Pinky shouted.

And he kicked the tree with all his might.

The tree shook, and snow fell, covering Pinky from top to bottom. But Pinky didn't notice. He had other things on his mind:

Mushrooms, mozzarella cheese,
Fresh tomatoes, onions, peas.

Down the road, the Skunk sisters were building a snowman.

"*That* snowman is even better than ours," said one of the sisters.

What does she mean? Pinky wondered. But he was in too much of a rush to find out.

Mushrooms, mozzarella cheese,
Fresh tomatoes, onions, peas.

On Main Street, Pinky saw Mr. and Ms. Wagner and their boy Ben. He saw Mrs. Schnauzer and Mr. Mutton. All of them were abuzz with excitement.

"A walking snowman!"
he heard them say.
Where? Pinky wondered.

Beaver's Bakery

Pinky turned the corner and heard again, "A walking snowman!"

Pinky looked all around him. *Where? Where?*

Outside the bakery, Mr. Withers, Ms. Muzzle, Mr. Digger and even the baker himself were talking about the snowman.

And in front of the pharmacy, Officer Barker reported the walking snowman to headquarters.

Pinky wanted to see the snowman too, but he didn't have a moment to spare. He had reached the pizzeria at last!

Pinky rushed in and shouted,
*"Mushrooms, mozzarella cheese,
Fresh tomatoes, onions, peas."*

One of the Coniglio twins was so startled he dropped his dishes! "A walking, talking snowman!"

Pinky didn't even notice.
*"Mushrooms, mozzarella cheese,
Fresh tomatoes, onions, peas."*

Mr. Coniglio laughed.
"A pizza-pie snowman!"

Recognizing the pink little snout, Mr. Coniglio went to the kitchen to make Pinky's pizza.

MACY

And while Pinky waited in the warm room, the snow that surrounded him started to melt.

By the time the pizza was ready, the snowman was all gone. . . .

And a wet little boy stood in its place.

PIZZERIA

Pinky ran as fast as a small boy with a large pizza could.

"Did you see the walking snowman?" asked Mr. Mutt as Pinky went by.

Home in a flash, Pinky proudly delivered the pizza to Mommy.

PIZZA

It had . . .
Mushrooms, mozzarella cheese,
Fresh tomatoes, onions, peas . . .

and it was still hot.

And after their delicious lunch, Pinky and Mommy took a stroll into town. They wanted to see the walking snowman too!

Books

To my friends who are far away in snowy Moscow

Printed and Bound in April 2016 at Tien Wah Press, Johur Bahru, Johur, Malaysia.
The artwork was created with watercolors, gouache and ink.
www.holidayhouse.com
First Edition
1 3 5 7 9 10 8 6 4 2

Library of Congress Cataloging-in-Publication Data
Names: Gorbachev, Valeri, author, illustrator.
Title: Pizza-pie snowman / Valeri Gorbachev.
Description: First edition. | New York : Holiday House, [2016] | Summary:
"Running through town to get a pizza for himself and his mother, Pinky
unwittingly becomes covered in snow; now everyone thinks he is a walking
snowman!" — Provided by publisher.
Identifiers: LCCN 2015045403 | ISBN 9780823436545 (hardcover)
Subjects: | CYAC: Pizza--Fiction. | Snow—Fiction. | Mothers and
sons—Fiction. | Animals—Fiction. | Humorous stories.
Classification: LCC PZ7.G6475 Pi 2016 | DDC [E]—dc23 LC record available at http://lccn.loc.gov/2015045403

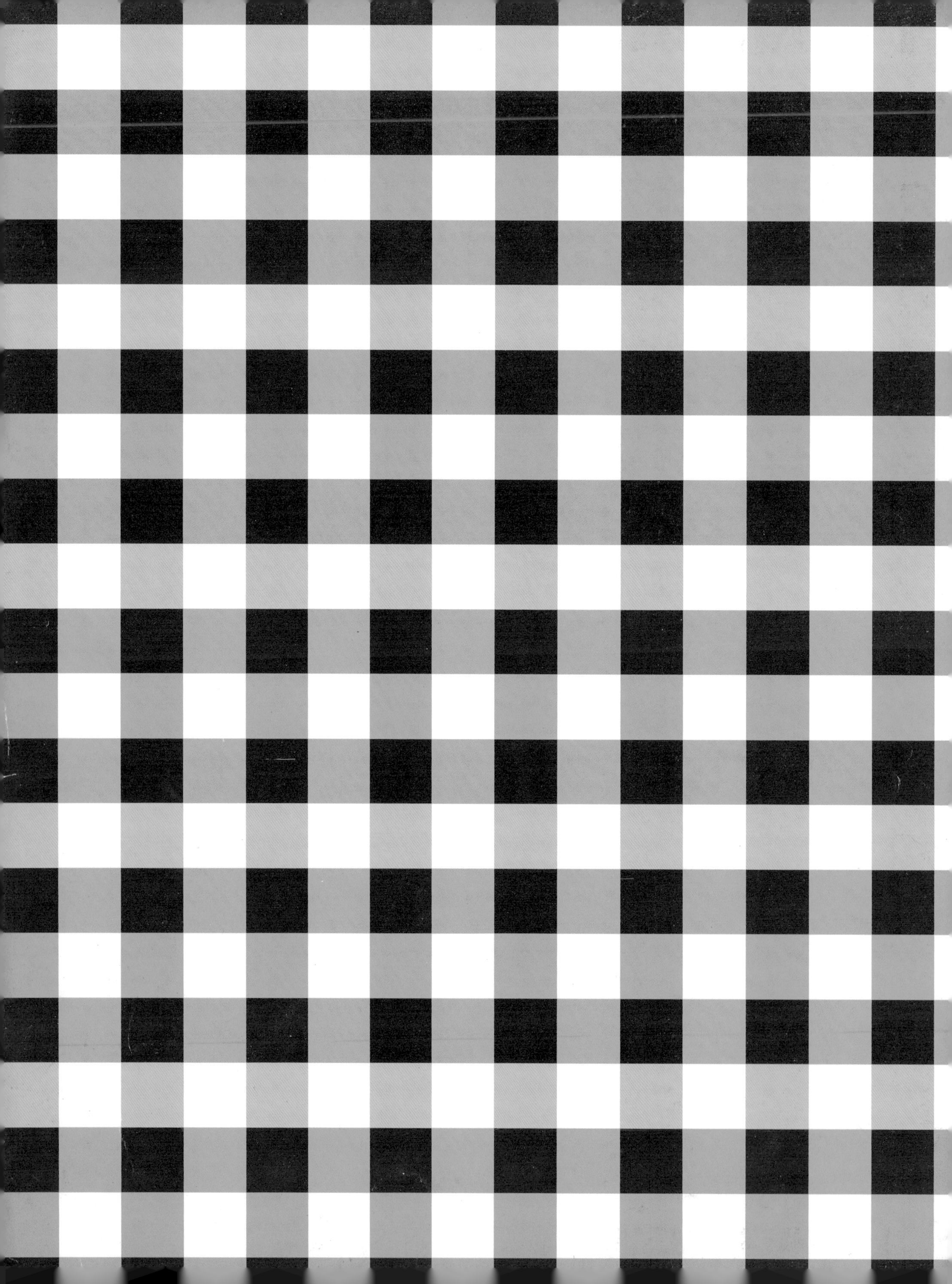